Alph. Hamilton Wood

**Abraham Lincoln**

A Drama

Alph. Hamilton Wood

**Abraham Lincoln**
*A Drama*

ISBN/EAN: 9783337341640

Printed in Europe, USA, Canada, Australia, Japan

Cover: Foto ©Andreas Hilbeck / pixelio.de

More available books at **www.hansebooks.com**

# ABRAHAM LINCOLN,

# A DRAMA,

—BY—

## ALPH. HAMILTON WOOD, A. M.

LAMAR, MO.
MISSOURIAN BOOK AND JOB OFFICE,
1883.

# ABRAHAM LINCOLN.

## ANALYSIS.

This historical drama comprises a period of four years and two months, beginning February 21, 1861, and ending with the capture and death of the assassin Booth, April 20, 1865.

In the autumn of 1860 occurred the regular election of President of the United States. The great political question Slavery was the strong plank in the platform of all parties ; and when it was ascertained that the Anti-slavery or Northern States had elected Abraham Lincoln to the office, the Pro-slavery or Southern States began to declare their secession from the mother-government.

In February, about a month before Lincoln was to be inaugurated, the states which had seceded called a convention at Montgomery, Alabama, proclaimed their independence, and formed themselves into the government of the "Confederate States," the two chief officers of which were Jefferson Davis, and Alex. H. Stephens. Quickly following this date, began the private plottings, and the four years' civil war from which are taken the incidents of the play.

## DRAMATIS PERSONÆ.

ABRAHAM LINCOLN, Pres. of the U. S.
JEFFERSON DAVIS, Pres. of the C. S.
ALEX. H STEPHENS, V.-Pres. of the C.S.

U. S. GRANT, General to Lincoln.
R. E. LEE, General to Davis,
J. W. BOOTH, Lincoln's Assassin.

THOMPSON
SANDERS,
CLEARY,
CLAY,
TUCKER,
} Friends to Davis ; and Booth's Assistant Conspirators.

GREGORY, Aid to Davis.

BEAUREGARD,
EWELL,
BOWEN,
MONTGOMERY,
} Generals assistant to Davis.

McPHERSON,
BURNBRIDGE,
WEITZELL,
} Generals assistant to Lincoln.

BENJAMIN,
WALKER,
} Members of Davis's Cabinet.

ATZEROTH,
HAROLD,
PAYNE,
MRS. SURRATT,
} Accomplices to Booth.

DONALD, Aid to Lincoln.
TANEY, Chief Justice of U. S.

SEWARD,
CAMERON,
STANTON,
} Members of Lincoln's Cabinet.

ABBOTT, A Physician
GURLEY, A Minister.
HAWK, *alias* SQUILLS, An Actor.
LADY LINCOLN.
LADY DAVIS.

Citizens, Soldiers, Police, Attendants, Messengers, Ghosts.

# ABRAHAM LINCOLN.

## ACT I.

*Cleary.* Montgomery is no mean city ; -
The delegates to the Convention saw
That its adorning was their welcome ;
Last week no stone by it was left unturned
Which could contribute pleasure to its guests
At the Inaugural. Memorable day
When Davis took the rule of states seceding!

*Sanders.* And lucky day! just in the nick of time--
Ev'n in the Washingtonian month of *Nothings*,
Which by the calendar of politics,
Like leap-day, comes one year in four, and makes
A president a common citizen,
And common citizen a president.
I will repeat it,—just in the nick of time—
Too late to fear an action from Buchanan,
Too soon for Lincoln's coming government
To blow at us a blast of war. And war--
In truth all heads are bent on't—we may expect
Unless we can present so bold a front
That Lincoln dare not undertake it.
Advantages which might be taken now
Must not be overlooked ; to us 'tis spring
And favorable for our planting.

*Cleary.* The floating rumor of this afternoon
Once turned to fact, will give assistance then.

*Sanders.* Rumor? what rumor?—you lead me in the dark.

*Cleary.* You had not heard it ? Why this Rumor said,
"The *weed* would be upturned before the time
Of casting seed."—'Tis evident 'twas Lincoln.

*Sanders.*  It is no secret?

*Cleary.*                                    None, none in the least
The thought was cause for merriment and jest;
And then the conversation turned again
Upon some state affairs.

*Sanders.*  (*Meditatively.*)  The weed! the weed
Would be upturned before its casting seed—

*Cleary.*  Not quite!  Before its *time* of casting seed.

*Sanders.*  I understand.  Before the fourth of March
Lincoln will have his head lopped off --

*Cleary.*  Yes, yes.

*Sanders.*  I cannot credit it, though I may wish it.
To know the truth of it without a question
Suppose we eavesdrop through the street.

*Cleary.*                                    No, no,
Let's go to Thompson's—he can tell us more--

*Sanders.*  We'll go to Thompson's, yes! we'll through the park!
We'll eavesdrop!—three acts in one—ha, ha!          [*Exeunt.*

---

ACT I, SCENE II.  THOMPSON'S ROOM.

*Enter* THOMPSON, BOOTH *and* STEPHENS.

*Thompson.*  The vantage-ground is gained; the outset shows
That triumph even now pervades the air
That breathes o'er our Confederated States.

*Booth.*  And as calm air may quickly change to wind
So may these flattering signs be sped away.

*Thompson.*  Perhaps this air, averse to nature, then,
May cool the heated pulse of Northern men.

*Booth.*  Success you claim on easy terms.

*Thompson.*                                    'Tis here:
Buchanan at the Union pilot-wheel
Directs the Ship of State, and feigns to sleep
While we the Nation's banded troops dispose, ·

Transfer its men-of-war to distant seas,
Possess its forts, ope wide the treasury's mouth
And pour its store to a revolting South.

*Stephens.*  One word, a thought.  The presidential chair
A new incumbent has this very year,
Inaugurated on the fourth of March
Lincoln dethrones Buchanan, takes the crown,
Seceding rights denies, makes slavery vain,
Proclaims himself the chieftain, monarch, lord,
Of Union undivided—

*Thompson.*  Aha, he'd make a Rome of this fair land,
Himself dictator, despot arrogant.
Plebeian rank, low-bred Plebeian he,
Cradled in poverty, fostered in rags,
A brazen, saucy urchin, long-haired youth,
Oxgoader, woodman, wharf-fed roustabout,
Officious vender of another's ware,
Vain pettifogger, trifling orator,—
Now see! behold this mushroom mastodon
The god of an infuriated North—

*Stephens.*  Thompson, cease ranting.  Lincoln is my friend.
In Congress we were brothers, walked arm in arm,
Sat near together, entered joint debate ;
When votes were counted we alike were yea
Or nay ; as fell the evening's quiet shade,
In conversation pleasant hours we turned.
Of age well suited for companionship,
He proved himself free from hypocrisy,
Devoted to his cause, conservative,
Respected for his honor, for wisdom loved ;
A half a score of blissful years were passed
In this fraternity.  As branches twin
From the self-same trunk of a forest oak,
So we, when Right of Slavery was brought
Within the Senate Chamber, grew in two,
He leaning to the North, I to the South.
At first, apart we stood a hair in breadth,
But agitation gave a rapid growth
To politics—it was our nourishment—

Till now—four paltry years are passed—he takes
The highest seat his party can bestow
While I next to the highest hold from mine.
Justly we disagree. Call him no names;
America confers no dignity,
Title or excellence, because of birth;
Thou, he and I, began in life the same,
Stark naked, without preeminence.
Made he, himself, then greater honor's due
To his creation. 'Tis not he at fault
That our State's Independence must be gained
By force of arms; but all opprobrium
And ignominy, censure and reproach,
Must fall upon his party politic.

*Thompson.* The truth! the truth!
To guillotine a man brings instant death,
Likewise to kill a Party behead its chief
Sweet Liberty will come when Lincoln falls,
To hasten which, this is the instrument. (*Produces a pistol.*)

*Stephens.* O, leave off evil thoughts; far better be
The offspring of a prostituted mother
Than base assassin of a common brother.

*Thompson.* A wish expressed you take for serious fact.

*Stephens.* Would it were not a wish. Only to-day
The flush of youth was on thy cheek,
No angry frowns were knitted in that brow;
As pure as ever looked from infant face
Those eyes were sparkling sweet with innocence;
Now, now! a wicked heart—encased so fair—
And vile desires have made thee maniac,
Deprived thee of an open countenance;
Until with clench'ed hands, distended sight,
And grating teeth, thou makest bold to wish
A pistol's shot.

*Thompson.* Unsafe with me, *you* take the weapon.

*Stephens.* No, Thompson, no.
But let thy better part control thy worser,
Blur not thy conscience, nor a keen sense blunt

By any rash or inconsiderate act.

*Thompson.*  Bear no uneasiness.

*Stephens.*                              Reason's resumed,
Henceforth be honest to thyself—Good-night,
Till angel-dreams may smoother make thy temper,
Wiser thy brain, and worthier thy soul—
Good-night to both of you, good-night.          [*Exit.*

*Thompson.*                              Good-night.—
He is a man whom Equity has taught,
But what is Equity when civil war
Is pendant by a hair?  Thank fortune, Booth,
He's gone.—I'll move this folding-wall,
          (*Thompson rises, the scenery moves back, showing a park
          in rear.*)
And we shall go into the moon-lit park.
          (*They enter the park.*]
When was an eve more fair?

*Booth.*  Never.

*Thompson.*  The-moon one-quarter risen silvers
This pleasant grove inviting visitors.

*Booth.*  (*Turning to a bower*)
Here, see here.  Look you what some hand has wrought,
A woman's—

*Thompson.*  Aye, you guessed it right.
Let's seat ourselves and breath the balmy air.

*Booth.*  (*Sitting.*)  And do we stay?

*Thompson.*·                              A moment—'twill suffice
To hear brief history:—Montgomery
Appointed for Convention, numerous
As bees about a hive on swarming day,
Were volunteers to decorate the streets
And public walks.  Festoons of evergreen
O'er hanging arches, mottoes gilt with gold,
Pictures and statuary, were prepared
The usher of this new-born government.
The ladies sought this most secluded spot
Of all the park, designed and wrought this bower;
Beneath this double rustic chair was spread

A carpet of sweet-briar leaves, moss-pink,
And willow catkins, with unseen support
The ivy grew in air, the woodbine twined
And peeped its colors through ; encircling centres
Of *arbor vitae* wreaths with buds of rose
And violets enwoven made the dome
Where Venus. crowned with orange-blossoms, swung
In statue. Done, 'twas named Retreat of Lovers

*Booth.* (*Rising he takes Thompson's arm and makes him sit.
Booth stands.*) Then you yourself sit down, for we are lovers—
Lovers of country, Lovers of liberty—

*Thompson.* A footfall. Hush !

*Booth.* 'Tis your own heart ; if not. a rustling leaf.

*Thompson* Your speech ?

*Booth.* Stephens will favor no conspiracy ,
Fine precepts his when damned tyranny
An insurrection makes.

   *Thompson.*        That noise again!

*Booth.* Yes, forms of men beyond the second walk,
In this direction, here. 'Tis Tucker's gait,
And with him –

   *Thompson.*     Clay. I'll warrant—
His feet are always half a pace behind
His body ; body half its width behind
His comrade's—come.

*Booth.* (*Both advancing*) Not tardy thus his mind ; of it he makes
A mentor, and by it acquires his wealth.

      ( *Tucker and Clay approach.*)

*Thompson.* (*Lower*) To-night he uses a cane—

*Booth.*                     Or cudgel.

      ( *They meet.*)

(*At once.*)
   { *Thompson.* Good friend, how now ?
   { *Tucker.* In best of mood, proceeding—
   { *Booth.* Luckily we meet. (*He squeezes Clay's hand on shaking.*)
   { *Clay.* Thou hast the grip

    ( *Tucker's attention is arrested by Booth.*)

*Booth.* Indeed! my muscle *is* in tension held,
Also is Thompson's ; so would yours and yours (*to Tuck. and Clay*)
Have been had you but heard that speech.

*Tucker.* What speech?

*Booth.*                  Of Stephens.
He flattered Lincoln with deliberate tongue,
Upbraided Thompson, called him maniac
For wishing that some fatal accident
Might suddenly befall this would-be king—
Sir, 'twould have nerved a bony skeleton,
Clothed it with flesh, coursed it with blood, given it
An iron heart, keen sight, and steady hand
To shoot the dreaded despot—

*Clay.* (*Aside to Thompson*)
Man of small speech, is he beside himself?

*Booth.* He's of sound mind.—My ire is deeper stirred
The more I think. Our rights we must secure,
We will, if I may drop a leaden pill
Into *his* cup of fate—whose?—ask me not,
But make a hundred-thousand-dollar purse,
And I, as midwife to a bastard child,
Will deal a draught which knows no antidote.

*Tucker.* (*To Thomp. and Clay.*)
Shall we accept?

*Thompson.*         What if your scheme should fail?

*Booth.* By heaven, not so!

*Thompson.* It may be ; then—

*Booth.*                  The money's yours again.

(*Booth sits.*)

*Tucker.* (*To Clay*) What say you?

*Clay.*                Meet him here again to-night
At ten o'clock ; meantime consider well,
Counsel together and agree.

                [*Exeunt Thomp., Clay and Tucker.*

*Booth* (*Meditates and rises to leave.*)
A hundred thousand dollars buys the life
Of Lincoln!                   [*Exit.*

ACT I.  SCENE III.  THOMPSON'S ROOM.

*Enter* THOMPSON, CLAY *and* TUCKER.

*Clay.*  Depositors of banks examine first
The stock and state securities, then take
A check subject to order.  Business rules
Demand no less of him whom we employ;
Hence, show his character and company,
And mark what obligation makes him bound
To execute our will.

  *Tucker.*    He asks too large a purse.
       (*A servant enters.*)
  *Thompson.*   We'll seek advice
From Sanders, Young, and—Gregory—

  *Gregory.*  Sanders and Cleary ask the company
Of yourself, Clay, and Tucker.

  *Thomp.*  Bring them within to wait our readiness—(*Exit serv.*)
Cleary will fill the place of Young—

  *Tucker.*      And better.
    (*Enter Sanders and Cleary.*)
  *Thompson.*  Greetings to each of you--we are all friends.--
Last night ere slumber closed my eyes, and  stopped
My brain, I prayed that curses, like hoary frosts,
Might fall upon the heads of Northern men
To lay their leaders in befitting graves;
If Great Jehovah'd grant this heavenly boon,
By angel herald's I prayed he'd make it known.
Upon this couch I lay, and o'er me fell
The balm of sleep, till when I waked, 'twas morn;
The glorious sun on the horizon's rim,
Was shining through my window here, while there,
Upon the wall, right there, it wrought in great
And golden letters, "CONFEDERATED STATES."

  *Sanders.*  You are our seer, our prophet.  "God helps them
Who help themselves."  By means, not chance, He works;
The plan's unveiled, the secret's out, your dream
May be interpreted.

*Thompson*   Now?

*Sanders.*      Ay, even now!

*At once.*   { *Tuck.* What's the result? give the result.

     { *Clay.* Whence comes thy wisdom? Art thou a Daniel
More wise than all thy fellows?

*Sanders.* Misguided men, to think that oracles
Befit so rude a tongue. Yourselves compose,
Be undisturbed while I the fact disclose.

*Tucker.*    We're ready.

*Sanders.* From the Retreat this eve at eight I heard,
"A hundred thousand dollars buys the life
Of Lincoln."

*Thompson.* Where were you?

*Sanders.*     At its rear.

*Thompson.* Heard nothing more?

*Sanders.*    But footfalls of one departing.

*Clay.* Were those his words precisely?

*Sanders.*     Exactly.

*Thompson.* Unraveled!
    We left Booth there near striking hour;
He wanted money, but told us not for what,
Only that it would bring us liberty—
A man most cautious, thoughtfully determined,
True to his friends, his country and the cause
He has espoused—enough! what seek we more?
My vision spurs me on to give my means
To aid our righteous claim.

*Sanders.* If failing?

*Tucker.*   The money he returns.

*Thompson.* His honor's his security.

*Sanders.* Patriot blood is true.

*Clay.*                           Are we agreed?

*All*                             Agreed.

*Clay.* Cleary shall be the clerk, receive the funds,
And with appropriate words convey to Booth
At the Retreat to-night at ten.                    [*Exeunt.*

---

ACT I.  SCENE IV.  DAVIS'S CABINET, MONTGOMERY.
*Enter* DAVIS, *meditatively.*

*Davis.* That happy dream of youthful years  so full
Of sweet expectancy, when for my sword
No laurels left, I'd sit on throne of thrones;
Dream, dream, delightful dream, O bless'ed dream,
I little thought to see thee here so soon.
As Washington pursued the Indian trail,
Drove out the French, upheld the Royal Flag,
Then quickly turned against the mother-world,
· In revolution, gaining for himself
The title Father—Father of his country;
So I, I, yes I, even I, drove west
The painted foe; blood thirsty Mexicans
But for a look I killed; the Stars and Stripes
Tattoo'ed in my arm, showed loyalty;
Still climbing upward, (*patting his head*) here, here is the ladder
     (*Greg. enters and surprises Davis in his dream.*)
By which to fame I rise—Ho, Gregory!

*Gregory.* 'Tis nine o'clock and later.

*Davis.*                  Bring in my cabinet,
I'd talk with them before the hour of bed          [*Exit Greg.*]
To counsel with my cabinet what need
Have I?—Oh, ho, I'll work the wires and *they*
Shall be my puppets.
            (*Enter Cabinet.  Greg. reads news.*)
Uncommon times demand unusual hours,
But know the present shall not long detain you.
                  Selected ruler,
A wise administration I would make,
And to my aid I've summoned you, my friends,

In lull assurance that our cause is one.
If now a just perception of fair means
And mutual interests, permits our Party
Peaceably to pursue a separate
Political career. my earnest prayers
Are answered ; but this right of free-born men
Denied, and our integrity assailed,
Nothing remains but to appeal to arms
And crush the coming Monarchy which wears
The hateful stigma, "Lincoln Government."
Gregory !

    *Gregory.*    Your obedient servant.

    *Davis,*                        What news ?

    *Gregory.*    Lincoln harrangues at Independence Hall
To-morrow ; thence to Harrisburg, *en route*
To Washington.

    *Davis,*          Which way ?

    *Gregory,*               By Baltimore.

    *Davis.*    May *it* salute him as deserves his person—
                                        [*Exit Greg.*]
My Message to our first assembled congress
Must be prepared to meet emergencies
Of State, War. Treasury,—of all Departments,—  (*Clock strikes.*)
One-half to ten o'clock—each one take thought
How he may add a measure to his office ;
Your plans weigh well, and make me quick report.   [*Exeunt.*]

---

    ACT I.  SCENE V.  THE PARK AGAIN.
     *Enter* BOOTH, *whistling dolefully.*

    *Booth.*  They'll hear my whistling, if anywhere about.—
               (*Looks at his watch.*)
To meet them here at ten they said—not ten ?
The night drags slowly on ; and what a night,
What change from eight o'clock.
           (*Draws his overcoat.*)
                A northern blast,
A blizzard, cold as overtures of peace,

Freezes life's current 'fore it begins to flow,
(*Tightens his neckcloth.*)
This frosty air is eating at my lungs,
It makes my voice come huskily! a dram
Of Holland gin would give my system tone—
But no, I am a temperate man. My soul,
Take sustenance and warmth from fiery thoughts:—
The deed! the deed! I'll do it, though it put
My body to the rack. I'll be a Brutus
To thrust a dagger, say 'twas love for freedom,
And counterfeit a face of innocence.
Lincoln, I'll—not coming yet?—

(*Above and at the rear, on the rocks, an angel messenger appears.*)

*Messenger.* Booth! good Booth! most noble Booth!
Heaven descended messenger of Mars
I come to bless thy reverie, and swear
Thou art the man to seal a tyrant's doom.

(*Booth drops on his knees, toward the Mess. Cleary enters silently.*)

*Booth.* Most favored man I am! (*Mess. vanishes.*) My duty's
plain.

*Cleary.* Booth, friend Booth, thy mind disturbed?

*Booth* Saw nothing? Heard nothing?

*Cleary.* Nothing! nothing!
Hither I come with greeting from thy friends,
Who bid thee if a Gessler cross thy track
Shoot him to the heart; and take this purse
To make escape. Fare-thee-well, farewell. [*Exit.*

*Booth.* Commissioned by heaven, commissioned by men,
I'll hound him like a hare, and of my game
Make carrion. (*Leaving*) To Baltimore I haste —
(*Stopping.*) O Earth, and Rocky Steep, and Vaulted Sky,
Bear witness, (*Leaving.*) to-morrow is the day. (*Curt. drops.*)

# ACT II.

SCENE I.   EAST FRONT OF THE CAPITOL, WASHINGTON.

(*The scenery is the East Portico of the Capitol.*)

*Enter* CITIZENS.

*1st. Cit.*   Already what a crowd.

*2nd. Cit.*                 A holiday.

*3rd. Cit.*   A gala day.

*4th. Cit.*   One year in four makes leap-year day.

*5th. Cit.*   Buchanan leaps out, Lincoln leaps in;
Therefore it is a capital day—

*4th. Cit.*               Indeed,
A Capitol day indeed.   The portico
Of that grand edifice will bear at noon
The mettled spirit of a Washington—
Lincoln's Inaugural address we wait.

*1st. Cit.*   Despite assassins' threats our Lincoln lives
Like Abraham of old, chosen of the Lord.

*2nd. Cit.*   Justice and judgment are at his command;
As dawned this morning's gray, the well-known eagle
Which fled the city four years ago, returned,
Sailing the bosom of the air in rounds,
Successive rounds, lower and lower, nearer
And nearer Lincoln's lodgings; easily
Descending, poised with out-stretched wings, it stood
Most motionless above the flag which floats
Upon the building's front; then quietly
It rose in air, departing as it came.—

*5th. Cit.*   And still 'tis seen encircling in the sky.

(*Gen. Scott, behind the scenes, speaks through a trumpet.*)

*Scott.*   Stand guards, on either side!

{ *Soldiers with guns, appear on each side of stage; an officer* }
{ *steps out and points citizens into the audience; music at rear.* }

*Officer.*  Make room in front! Withdraw into the crowd!

(*Citizens disperse; heavy music in front and rear.  Enter on
Portico,* LINCOLN, TANEY, *Officers of State, Senators, &c.*)

*Lincoln.*  Fellow Citizens of the United States:
Time-honored custom makes formalities
To which I cheerfully comply, most sacred.
Questions of little moment I'll defer.
Among the men of Southern States, exists
An apprehension that, because of change
To a Republican Executive,
Their property, peace and security
Will be endangered.  From public speech
I quote and still declare:--"With slavery,
In states where it exists, I have no purpose
To interfere."  While to *these*, as other states,
Protection will be meted equally
My predecessors, all distinguished men,
Fifteen in number, have administered
This branch of government, and generally
With great success conducted it through peril ;
Yet I, with all this scope for precedent,
Under peculiar difficulties enter
Upon the task.
The great disruption of the Federal Union,
Heretofore only menaced, is attempted
By grave secession.  No government
Has had provision in its primal law
To terminate itself.  Perpetuity
Is the fundamental principle of all
National governments.  Continue then
To execute our Constitution's will,
And Union forever stands.

But rights
Withheld without redress, provokes just cause
For revolution.  If to any one
A Constitutional right has been denied,
Let him speak.
            To hold, possess, and occupy
The Nation's property, and to collect
Its duties, constitutes my use of power ;

Bloodshed shall not be known, unless forc'd upon
The National authority.  Think well!
Let patriotism and calm intelligence,
Christianity, and Him above, adjust
Our present difficulties.  Your own hands,
My discontented fellow-countrymen,
Not mine, hold the great issue of civil war.
The government will never make the attack.
No conflict you can have, unless yourselves
Are the aggressors.  In Heaven's register
You have no oath recorded to destroy
The government, while I the solemn one
Shall have, to preserve, protect, defend it.
  I'm loath to close.    We are not enemies.
Though passion may have strained, it must not break
Our bonds of love.  Memory's mystic chords,
Stretching from every battle-field and grave
Of patriot, to every living heart
And hearth-stone over this broad land, will swell
Once more the happy chorus of the Union,
When touched again, as surely they will be,
By the better angels of our natures.

*(Heavy music while Lincoln receives the oath administered by Chief
Justice Taney.  Music so loud as to drown the words of the oath.)*

### THE OATH.

By oath I solemnly affirm that I
Will execute most faithfully the office
Of President of the United States,
And to the best of my ability
Preserve, protect, defend its constitution.        [*Exeunt.*

---

ACT II.  SCENE II.  STREET. EAST FRONT OF CAPITOL.

*Enter* BOOTH.

*Booth.*  Why were those soldiers standing there ?  Who knows ?
Perhaps they keep the peace with bayonet points,
And mean to break it with the same—        [*Enter* THOMPSON.
            Good Thompson !
Ha !  You burst forth as from above !

*Thompson*               And you—
Still at your task ?

*Booth.*      I'm here in Washington.

*Thompson.*  And so is Lincoln.

*Booth.*           But would not be,
Had he not been a babe of timid birth,
And come before his time.  His friends alert
By early flight he stole through Baltimore,
Escaping thus the death he justly merits.
I tell you Thompson, in this I'll persevere
Even to persistency.

*Thompson.*          O noble Booth,
If more, like you, were great of principle,
Desp ts would fall, and tyranny would fail.
But I'm to intercept your work—

*Booth.*               And will
With flattery begin it ?

*Thomson.*         Noble one,
And honorable—

*Booth.*     Dress speech in plainer clothes !

*Thompson.*  'Tis not to irritate you that I talk :
But first to credit you a valorous man,
Then change your purpose—
*Booth.*          Change the heavens,
But my heart's purpose you'll never change !

*Thompson.*  I know that you aspire to liberty,—
Holy desire to which I am your comrade,
A goal from which I'd never see you turn :
Only defer the present *means*, my friend,
In view of easier, better, wiser action.
A wily plan is laid to net this bird
Before his office wings are fledged.
·*Booth.*           Most wise.

*Thompson*  And King-birds served are savory for gods.
*Booth.*  That word's your best.

*Thompson.*                    Commissioners of Peace,
Honey-mouthed men, will win the Prince with words.
Should he deny us separate government,
We'll rise, and overpower, and conquer him—

*Booth.*  That's easiest done !

*Thompson.*                    You shall be amply paid,
I'll see to it.—Your boldness makes you great :—
It ranks you with our zealous patriots ;
The fact ! it puts your name on honor's roll ;
It offers you a seat in Congress—

*Booth.*  I'll not accept it though  I'm for the stage,
There nightly I may thrust the keen-edged sword
Into the heart of kings, and watch them fall
To dead men's level.  I'll take to tragedy—
My honest trade—, and when your peace is failed
I warrant you relief by Lincoln's death—
Now come with me, and in some unseen attic
I'll count you back the money.                    [*Exeunt.*]

---

ACT II.  SCENE III.  CABINET ROOM, WASHINGTON.

*The "Capitol Scenery" opens, and the Cabinet room is thus shown.  LIN-
COLN and his CABINET are seen in consultation.*

*Lincoln.*  Respecting the Commissioners of Peace
My judgment is the same as yesterday ;
As influential men they may be heard
But not as diplomates.  Once recognized,
The independence of the government
Which Southerners assume, is then conceded.

*Seward.*  When first these men arrived at Washington
By Chair of State was this advisement made.
Now, much deliberation wastes itself –
Forsyth and Crawford took their leave to-day,
This letter just received imparts their purpose.

*Lincoln.*  Conciliation by pacific means
Is preferable to force.  With angry men
Passion is emperor which to speak against
Is putting flame to Reason's tinder-pyre ;

But thoughtful words with help divine, will slay
That soulless demon except what Fancy bears
When wed with love of Fame. Therefore, my men,
Let Heaven's Sovereign inspire your motives
And mildness characterize your words: e'en still
Contract they war, the same Almighty Throne
Rightly may be invoked to our defense.
But to evacuate our Nation's forts,
As they desire of Sumpter, we have no right;
Not more of right to give strongholds to them
Than to some foreign power. Formerly
Charlestown mart provisioned Anderson;
Yesterday, orders passed from Beauregard
Who heads eight thousand rebels in the seige,
Prohibiting all further intercourse—
Cameron, what peaceful course will give relief?

*Cameron.* To brave no dare, yet to defend our trust,
Let unarmed vessels carry food to Sumpter.

*Lincoln.* I give accord, Dispatch the word.—Perhaps
This modest way may make rebellion cease.　　　　[*Exeunt.*

------

ACT II. SCENE IV. DAVIS'S CABINET ROOM.

DAVIS *enters holding a winecup in his hand.*

*Davis.* The steed that bears a heavy load, betimes
Must lave his tongue in fountain stream;
Betimes he lags, the rider spurs a spur
That for a day requires no repetition:
To man, both pleasure and necessity
Meet in the sparkling cup of ruby wine—
It quenches thirst and stimulates the brain. 　　(*Sets cup down.*)
With shadowed eve comes smallest requiem
When with myself I counsel. This suspense
Which Lincoln's Government affects to ours
By treating our Commissioners of Peace
With answers si'nister, avers deceit, 　　(*Enter* GREGORY.)
It means——Gregory!

*Gregory.* Without are Benjamin and Walker.

*Davis.*   Bid them enter.—The Black Republicans
Will quickly find coercion is a plant
Not genial yet to Democratic soil.—

(*Enter* BENJAMIN *and* WALKER.)

Good men, most welcome.

*Benjamin.*               Not welcome thus
The news we bring.   Returned from Washington
Are Forsyth and Crawford, who a month were there
Without a hearing—officially denied.
Now it remains us to retrace our steps,
Retract our words, and hope in legislation,
Or by our nod induce a war.   Well said,
How few our numbers—

*Davis.*               Oh, faint heart thou hast!
I thought thy spirit was of better stuff—

*Benj.*   Nay, Davis, Nay ; you caught me up too soon,
How few our numbers, but what dauntless courage !   '
Our far extended plains, our woods, our rocks,
Our hills, our mountains, make of every man
A mighty Nimrod ; our homely jeans, our rice.
Our corn, our raw bear's meat and venison,
Make Spartans of us all.

*Davis.*               Yes, yes.   If Northerners
This land invade to set our negroes free,
Thermopylæs will beat them back, and give
          (GREG. *enters, giving a message to* WALKER.)
Their corses to the wind.—A message ?
*Walker.*   Lincoln orders Sumpter to be provisioned
By unarmed vessels ; but, *to be provisioned.*—
And Beauregard 'waits your direction.

*Davis.*   Instruct him to demand evacuation ;
If 'tis refused, he may reduce the fort.

*Walker*   I'll make him speedy answer.               [*Exit,*

*Davis.*                    Done, 'tis done,
Lincoln's pacific policy is done !
This blow once struck, accelerates our growth,
And adds new States to our confederation.               [*Exeunt.*

### ACT II. SCENE V. Fort Sumpter.

*(Scenes open and at the rear is seen the Fort.  Second morning of the battle; guns are heard; alarm.)*

*Enter* Beauregard *and* Officers.

*Beau.*  Messenger, haste, make haste to Cumming's Point,
To set her rifled guns.—And onward *then*     [*To mess. No. 2.*]
To Sullivan's Isle to work columbiads.—
To-morrow morn, that holy Sabbath morn,
Shall hear the pulpit pray and preach the praise
Of Beauregard.                    [*Enter* Messenger.

*Mess.*  On Morris Island's side the walls are falling—

*Beau.*  Speed thy return a victory to proclaim
Within an hour —My floating battery
Heaps honor to itself with every shot.—

*Soldiers.*  (*Behind scenes.*)  Ho, ho! the fort's again on fire,
                    (*The Fort burns.*)

*Officer.*  The flag's half-mast—they're in distress.

*Beau.*  Assistance send, but tardily.

*Officer.*  No, no! they strike their colors now.
                    (*cheering; bells ring; music.*)
*Beau.*  Let Major Anderson come forth.—Brave man,
I'll treat him easily, lest ire
Enkindled once in Lincoln's livid heart,
Appease its appetite with sweet revenge.
    (*Approach Anderson and guard.  Anderson surrenders his sword, which Beau. returns.*)
Thy sword I give thee back.  Depart in peace ;
Take transport for New York, and, sailing off,
Salute thy flag with fifty guns.                    [*Exeunt.*

---

### ACT II. SCENE VI. A Public Place.

*Enter* Lincoln.

*Lincoln.*  My countrymen, my federal countrymen :
Look you, look you toward the noonday sun
Where fields are gathering with hostile men,

And say forbearance longer is no crime ?
Behold there seven states opposing law
By league too powerful to be suppressed
By any ordinary course ; therefore,
These combinations to subdue, that laws
May find an execution, let all militia-men
Come forth obedient to this call.
United lovers, reaffirm your love ;
Put on your coats of mail ; do my command,
And seek redress for wrongs too long endured.—
I wait reply.                              [ *Curtain drops.*
(*Great noise. Responses from each side behind the scenes.
Music.*)

*Responses.* "We come !"   "Ten thousand strong we
come !"   "A hundred thousand more !"   "Union forever."

---

# ACT III.

### SCENE I. WASHINGTON. CABINET ROOM.

*Enter* SEWARD *and* STANTON.

*Seward*   Stanton, to-day how stands our army ?

*Stanton.*   Procrastination is a hopeless word,
McClellan is its late coined synonym—
From vain excuse he will refuse to act.
A year is past since he succeeded Scott,
And adulation crowned him "Young Napoleon ;"
His appellation now is "Little Mac,"
Or "Old Delinquency ;" his history
Repeats itself upon that bulletin,
    (*In view is a bulletin marked :* "*Sept 22. All quiet on the
    Potomac*".)
Read it and pray the gods to carve these words
In epitaph upon his tomb.
                              The West
By drawn engagements, quits a field ungained.
The fortunes of Missouri are reversed,
Kentucky's overpowered by rebel Bragg,
While Grant the Southern States to Union holds

Merely by force of arms.

*Seward.*                    Discouragement
Has greater been than now. Hast ever thought
What aid would come from slavery's abolition?

*Stanton.* I'm not an abolition's man, except
To save the Union.—Years since, my sympathy
Was with the South. I plead that slavery
Should be abandoned by purchase of the slaves;
But when those states were not amenable
To laws they helped to make, and in hot haste
Secession came, as if minority
Should rule; when from the bosom of our flag
The stars were plucked, and stripes were changed to bars;
When later, thousands were in arms against
This grand Republic,—I urged the President
To make slaves free by proclamation.

*Seward.* 'Tis evident no compromise will do.
The Carolinas' rice and cotton fields
And Louisiana's sugar-cane plantations
Will finally be tilled without the slave,
While Charleston's and New Orleans' streets become
The marts for merchandise legitimate;
Or, Massachusetts and New York must yield
The culture of their fields of growing grain
Unto the Blacks, while Boston and New York
License once more the hammering auctioneer
To trade in bodies and in souls of men,—
Slave-holding or free labor must be law
In all the states alike both North and South.
As thou art Stanton, and Seward I. I swear
That slavery admitted the Union dies,
But slavery abolished the Union lives.

*Stanton.* The step is in advance and should be urged —
Since Lincoln likes your counsel, advocate
Emancipation stronger than e'er before,
Tell him that thousands wait this one great act,
To rush around his standard; tell him, too
That here is hinged our Nation's unity;
And tell him this, that all the North, like us,
Is hot for abolition. You see to it—

He comes—you talk with him and mark his words.   [*Exit.*

*Enter* LINCOLN.

(SEWARD, *at the rear is not noticed.*)

*Lincoln.*  On civil seas this Nation is adrift
Wrecking itself upon an angry tide
Which ebbed in fullest heat the very day
I gripped the wheel.  It is intriguing Treason
Who sits upon the stern, who bred distrust
And prosecutes the war, sole cause of tempest;
Ah, yes, he is a wicked, godless Jonah
Whom bound I'll fling into the ocean's mouth,
And in the bowels of that briny deep
With penitence I'd hear him vow obedience.
My soul! the *thought* is good; but such an *act*
Belongs to Great Jehovah.  Some milder means
Must serve my purpose.—I bethink myself
Of the stout son—an aged father's staff:
Or him betrothed to some pure maiden's heart,
Or the sweet home where husband wooed the wife
With innocence a-prattling on his knee,—
All sacrifices, fresh-burnt offerings
Upon a Nation's altar.  I bethink myself
Of these, and justice melts to mercy.

   The traitors, led by wily men, are weak,
And weakness calls for mercy, calls for pity.
In my Inaugural I asked of them
That they be peaceable, and I'd protect
Their property.  Scorning my request,
Contemptuously they spurned the government;
Rebelliously they rose, and with stiff necks
Disdained my proffered treaties which, at times,
Were, Pardon in exchange for Loyalty,
Money to buy their slaves—sufficient money
To replace all damages.  They laughed!
They mocked my words!  They said, "Peace, peace,
We'll have no peace, no peace with Lincoln!"
O, Lincoln, patience is no more a virtue.
The time is come to lay their country waste,
To make their Negroes free, to spare them nothing—

                            (*Draws up his papers.*)

Well, shall I set my hand to it?--my name

Attached, and slavery will be abolished.
It is their dearest idol, their choicest treasure—
No, I repent ; too soon—too soon—

   *Seward,*                        For what,
When all your Party ask it?     ( *Lincoln speaks presently.*)

   *Lincoln.*                   Right outweighs
Desire, and both are naught when destitute
Of force to back them. No way mismatched
The armed contestants stand rivals of strength,
Though o'er the graves where martyred heroes lie
There rustle now the second autumnal leaves.

   *Seward.* This second year brings deeper contest, true,
But must the war be endless as eternity?
Secession's pretexts grew from slavery
Which binds the race of Ham to servitude
Most menial ; broken once these servile chains
By proclamation. Rebellion finds its end,

   *Lincoln.* More confident of this, I'd make the trial—
   *Seward.* Besides, if we had further need of soldiers,
As Stanton says, thousands would volunteer
Where none come now. From the committee-men
Who wait upon you daily, you know full well
The solid North is ripe for Abolition.

   *Lincoln.* That rebellion's a slave-holders' enterprise
I easily perceive. I, too, concede
Emancipation would help us at the North,
Though not so much, perhaps, as you may think.
The Union is to save, and in its saving
No course should be adopted which will decrease
The Union sentiment—which will result
In giving Border States unto the Rebels.
The feeling to preserve the Union whole
Is stronger than it was a year ago,
Stronger to-day than yesterday ; and when
This fundamental principle prevails,
When not the solid North alone, but *all*
Are ripe for Abolition, I'll publish then
The proclamation which is already written.—

   *Seward.* Written?

*Lincoln.*            Written was my word.  'Tis in the case,
Examine, and returning bring it.          [*Exit* SEWARD.
Donald:   The file of evening papers.—

  *Donald.*  Yes.  Of importance this.  A printed letter.
                (*Donald points to it in the N. Y. Tribune.*)

  *Lincoln.*  From whom?

  *Donald.*  From Greeley.  Read it?

  *Lincoln.*  Please you read.          (*Donald reads.*)

  *Donald.*  Mr. President:

From east to west by ocean limited
The fervent prayers of twenty millions souls
Invoke thy Majesty to see how false
Would be that peace which makes Rebellion stop,
But upholds Slavery—pausing to sleep,
Rebellion's strength would be renewed by morn,
As every champion of the Union knows.
  Ask your embassadors, ask them I say,
If your subservience to slave-holders' claims
Isn't the despair of statesmen!  Be admonished!
  The millions of your loyal countrymen
Demand an execution of the laws—
The Confiscation Laws,—by which advantage
Openly and ungrudgingly proclaim
Freedom to every slave—

  *Lincoln.*            I'd see it, sir
  (LINCOLN *takes the paper and reads.*  DONALD *withdraws.*)
This letter claims attention.  Perplexing theme,
Were Washington or Adams, Jefferson
Or Henry here, we'd meet thee eye to eye!
    (*He refers to a manuscript on the table.*)
I have it—Add a line or two, erase a word
Or substitute a better—what's easier done—
         MRS. LINCOLN *enters.*
There, there! this answer fits him to a dot
    (MRS. L. *puts her hand on his shoulder.*)

  *Mrs. Lincoln.*  My husband.

  *Lincoln.*            Mary, wife—my darling wife!
Your fairy steps unheard, you startle me.

*Mrs. L.* Too much absorbed you were with thought you mean.

*Lincoln* Perhaps. But sit ; I'd have you near– ay, near.—
Your hand is plump as when on bridal day
'Twas held in mine ; you've had a mother's care –

*Mrs. L.* More than a mother's care there's been to you ;
Daily you overwork. I find you weary,

*Lincoln.* You weary too, because you worry dear,--
I *would* not *have* you worry.

*Mrs. L.*                    Nor I—I *would* not *have*
A government ; I would not wage a war ;
I would not be a widow,--vain wishes

*Lincoln.* See, I am here—you're not, you're not a widow.

*Mrs. L.* I am! I am! this mansion makes me such.
You hold honor ; eh ? You hold drudgery,
And I hold robbery—I'm robbed of home,
Of vows, of company--

         *Lincoln.*              But not of love—

*Mrs. L.* Yes, robbed of love. Concealed within this cage—
This spacious cell—I find you only when
The prison-door's ajar. Unguarded once
You chance to peep into the open air
Some profligate will make of you a corpse :
This war has brought you enemies ; know you
To what proportions it has grown ? no stream
Or mountain brook within a Southern State
That has not stained itself with human gore.
O husband, did our God avenge his slain
By taking from our arms our darling child,
Our brightest son, our sweetest joy--our Willie ?
Think how a year ago our hearts were grieved,
And lest affliction spare us not again,
Forbear continuance of this cruel war,
Concessions make, find terms, secure the peace.

*Lincoln.* My christian queen, my wedded pride, my wife,
In truth not willingly neglected thou,
But neccessarily.--Your husband's words
Must comfort many broken-hearted wives,
His hand protect a nation's orphan world—

Children not blest as Willie, who lives a gem
In yonder realm: I am *your* solace too;
Heart, weep no more; by quickest means I'll save
Tthe Union, save our homes—'tis paramount
           (*Enter* SEWARD *unseen.*)
To save the Union, the other comes in course.
This end to gain, I'd make the negro free;
I think 'tis right—the only way there is
      (*Enter ghosts of* WASHINGTON *and* HENRY.)
To permanence—who's this! who's that! this! that!

     *Mrs. L.*   Where?

     *Lincoln.*         There.

     *Mrs. L.*           There's vacancy, there's nothing sir;
Is this a haunted room of bedlam ghosts?
You're ill, my lord, you're ill—your brain much crazed
With stubborn thought does court an apparition.
          (GHOSTS *vanish.*)

     *Lincoln.*   Woman, have apparitions eyes to see you.
And heads to nod at you? (*Seward makes noise*) Donald!

     *Seward*   'Tis I—

     *Lincoln.*        O! Seward, Seward—you, O Seward?

     *Seward.*   Yes, Lincoln, 'tis I—
The same as you, I saw two men
Age'd and courtly, brave patrician stock,
Countenances fresh as of a spirit-world
Where immortality adds purity
To virtue's glow, and makes the face its mirror,
Gives eyes their lustre, hangs the shoulders o'er
With curls more snowy than Imperial Jove's,
Adorns--        (GHOSTS *re-enter.*)

     *Lincoln.*   Again they come—they smile--

     *Mrs. L*   They beckon you—I pray you speak to them!

     *Lincoln.*   Ye spectral forms, precursors of some ill,
Or harbingers of love,—what would ye?

     *Ghost IV.*   *I* am thy country's father; *he*
It's first-born orator whose eloquence
Did *fire* men's foes to "liberty or death."

     *Ghost II.*         He by wise command
Did *lead* these men to liberty, not death.

The sword aside, directed he the loom
That wove this web of nations. Upon his head
He wore the crown, his hand the sceptre bore—
A lov'd and loving king, a President :
Rightful successor thou. He made the Union,
Thou must preserve it.

*Ghost W.*                Mischief foreseen,
I prayed for slavery's *gradual* abolition —

*Ghost II.*  And now, mischief at hand,
We pray for slavery's *speedy* abolition.       [*Vanish Ghosts.*]

*Lincoln.* Gone—gone. The paper!
(*Seizing it from Seward, he signs it, and rising proclaims:*)
                                January next
To every slave gives freedom !                 [*Exeunt.*

---

ACT II. SCENE II. VICKSBURG. FRONT OF BURNBRIDGE'S TENT.

Plan. { *Left Front—Union Camp and Tent of Burnbridge.* }
      { *Right Rear—Partial street-scene of Vicksburg.* }

*Enter* SOLDIERS—*aside, and* BURNBRIDGE.

*1st Sol.* Forty-five days Vicksburg has lived in siege.

*2d Sol.* But wall-eyed Famine forces her at last
To hoist the flag of white upon her front—

*1st Sol.* It leaves her stores as blank as cartridge-pods,
And tells a surer knell than leaden hail—

(*Enter* 3D SOLDIER—MIKE O'FLANNIGAN—*with a bound*)

*3d Sol.* Ho, Jeems, Jeems, ye're right now, ye're right, ye're right.
It bates the makin' o' paddies of ye chaps
Who's niver a paddy at all, at all ;
Who never shoveled one spadeful of dirt
In all the time before when ye was born ;
And Jeems, it aven bates ye'r Gineral
Who was so crazy afther a canal
To turn the Gulf into the Mississippi
On purpose jist to see his gunboats float
Adown the stream up to St Louis.
In faith! I'll tell ye, byes, Famine's a ruff,
He's been to Cork, and he's no gintleman —
He drinks the soup, an' ates the bones besides,

He dont lave manners in America ;
But why condemn a man ye niver saw,
An' no desire to make acquaintances ?

> (*He rummages his pockets.*)

*2d Sol.* I say, Mike, do you know what day this is ?

*3d Sol,* Bad luck ! what cares an Irishman for days
When his meerschaum is lost ?—niver a bit.
By the St. Patrick ! here he is—the pet
(*Produces a common clay pipe, and prepares to smoke.*)
The likes of me would take a dacent smoke
To warm up a cold breakfast on a hot
An' sultry summer mornin'. If ye'd know
What day it is, thin answer this *skanundrum.*

*1st Sol.* (*Laughing at him.*) This what !

*3d Sol.*          Skanundrum !—Och, Jeems, be still—
Would ye laugh at a poor old Irish galoot
Who has no ither friend but his meerschaum,
And his shillalah, an' gun, an' Biddy alone
With six or eight or tin childhren ?

> (*In joy he dances a sharp jig, whirling his shillalah upon his thumb.*)

Hurra'y ! Good luck to the world that was born
With *one* father an' niver a muther at all,
But ah, bad luck to the world that was born
On the Fourth of July with *many* fathers ♦
An' niver a muther at all, at all, at all !

> (McPHERSON *enters, and stamping his cane, the soldiers withdraw. He proceeds to give orders.*)

*McPherson.* Burnbridge, Grant designates your tent the place
To hear the embassy from Pemberton.
With blindfold eyes they come—you answer them.

> (*Enter* GEN. BOWEN *and* COL. MONTGOMERY, *blindfolded. They are led by two Union soldier guards.*)

*Guide.* Here is your place--speak to *him.*

*Bowen.*                              To whom ?

*Burnbridge.* To Burnbridge—I am he.

*Bowen.*                              To you ? To you ?
My message is to Grant—from Pemberton.

*Burnbridge.* My orders, sir, are positive.

*Bowen.* Then, sir, *mine*
Are negative—I will not speak with you—
Outside the picket-line is Pemberton
(*Exit* McPHERSON *to find* GRANT.)
Whom Grant himself may hold a parley with.
My guides, back to the front conduct us!
(*Guides come forward and lead them out. The soldiers
immediately reappear.*)

*1st Sol.* That messenger's a Johnny through and through
Without reduction—

*3d Sol.* But want of pork an' beans
Will bring redookshun though, right soon, d'ye mind?

*2nd Sol.* Mind nothing of the kind, but tumble down
Upon the ground till I set off this squib
(*He throws up fire-crackers which burst in air. 2d
Soldier sits. They fire their squibs rapidly.*)

*1st Sol.* Oh yes! we'll all be boys again, oh yes!
The 4th will recognize itself with these.
(*A bunch of lighted crackers are thrown under the feet
of 3d soldier.*)

*3d Sol.* Be aisy wid yerselves how ye rejoice!
(*He dances a jig, whirling his shillalah on his thumb.
Then he sings. The others fire their squibs.*)

SONG.
1   My name is Mike O'Flannigan,
      They call me Mike O'Flue,
  My father was an Irishman,
      But I'm a Yankee true.
            (*He dances another jig.*)
2.  My name is Mike O'Flannagin,
      They call me Mike O'Flue,
  I'm borne in ould Connecticut,
      And I'm a Yankee true,
  (*Cannons boom. Hurrahing on every part of the stage.
  1st and 2d soldiers spring to their feet.*)

*1st Sol.* Heigh-ho! heigh-ho!
*All.* (*Everywhere on stage*) Hurrah! hurrah! hurrah!
  (*These three soldiers join in the last two cheers.*) [*Exeunt.*

*Enter* GRANT, OFFICERS *and* SOLDIERS.

*Grant.*  My soldiers ! soldiers of this siege :

To-day,

This Independence Day, this glorious Fourth,
Vicksburg to you her knee in suppliance bends.
By art impregnable this stronghold stood
With countenance as indurate as steel,
Till you, brave men, about her sat ; this hour
I lead you forth her victors.  Plant once more
Our colors on her streets.  Renew your hearts,
That now Rebellion's master-piece is fallen.

(*Army flourishes on the stage.  Great noise—cheering.
Cannon, music, etc., behind the scenes.*)

SOLDIERS SING.--*Two parts.*

*1st Part.*  "We'll rally round the Flag, boys,"
*2d Part,*  Oh Vicksburg, Vicksburg's taken boys,
*1st Part.*  "We'll rally once again,"
*2d Part.*  Oh Vicksburg's taken, boys,
*All.*  "Shouting the Battle-cry of Freedom
Hurrah, boys, hurrah."  |*Curtain drops with the last singing.*

---

# ACT IV.

SCENE I.—DAVIS' RICHMOND.  CABINET ROOM.

(*Davis is busy at his desk.  A great rumbling noise
in the streets.*)

*Enter* MRS. DAVIS

*Davis.*  Returned from the Library, are you wife?

*Mrs. D.*  Yes, dear, for writing has no charms for me
When I must hear the battle's angry roar
From Petersburg, and see in Richmond here
Upon the streets a multitude of scared men
With frightened, crying women at their heels.

(*Great noises in street again.*)

*Davis.*  What's all that noise about ?

*Mrs. D.*                          Oh, that is it—
The great excitement ;—Some are throwing house-goods
In the streets that they may superintend

The bon-fire of their furniture ; some throw
The street into the house, and lock it there,
That they find abundance on return ;
Some shout—"The Yankees come"—"Are bound to come"—
"Lee can't much longer hold them back ;" some say
Farewell to friends, and run—run anywhere ;
Some pout, some mope about, some cry, some pray,
Some curse, and oh—There ! hear that noise again.
            (*Noise as before.*)

*Davis.*  And does my brave wife fear ?

*Mrs. D.*                                    Indeed I do !
Grant may take Richmond any day, and you
A prisoner, your life's not worth a groat.
The war is actually done.  You must give up,
You know it ; better take your chance in flight
And 'scape the city while you can.

*Davis.*  O my dear wife, are there no smiles behind
A frowning Providence ?  One-half the earth
Is always dark, yet light succeeds the darkness,
And that's the darkest hour next to the dawning ;
Thus, I have hoped that this's the breaking-forth
Of Independence morn, and Southern Freedom.

*Mrs. D.*  Your servants feed you weak anticipation,
And smooth your head with unctuous flattery.
Can you transform a zero to a unit ?
Why, you can never be a king, because
Your territory's taken —can't be a king
Because you have no subjects.  Save you your life
From yielding with the ruins of Confederacy.
You'll see sweet honor crown your silver locks
With the right-ruling of your household.
      Husband, if you love me come with me,
And Europe shall soon see us on her shore
Where we henceforth may dwell in peace.

*Davis*  Women are not, like men, for battle made ;
Still there is wisdom in your words, my love,—
You know we have a little honest cash,
A dozen millions, perhaps a little more—

*Mrs. D.*  Yes, the hard savings of your home and office—

*Davis.*  Well, it I ve buried,—directly in the drive
Ten steps beyond the door-yard spruce, and east.
Placed in an iron chest with well-brazed lid,
In ground and underneath the gravel road—
Such an unthought of place—the gold will keep '
Undisturbed, yellow and bright for many years.
When you have marked the place, you'll take the train
For Danville, accompanied by a guard of troops
Which I'll provide you—

 *Mrs. D.*     And leave you here?

 *Davis.*  Yes, for a day or two.  If there's no change
To favor Richmond soon, I'll follow you
And we will sail at once for Cuba.
Attend without delay, and I will go
With you a distance.       [*Exeunt.*
   *Enter* BENJAMIN *and* LEE.

 *Lee.*  The black and fated clouds of destiny
Hang like a pall o'er our Confederate States.
Since Vicksburg fell, defeat conjoins defeat—

 *Benj.*  And Lincoln fills his fetid soul with joy
To scent the carnage of the slain, while Grant
And Sherman, Sheridan and Farragut,
And more innumerable, engage his smiles
By deeds of conquest.

 *Lee.*    Our inefficiency
A separate political career
To gain, an independent government
To make, has proved itself by four years' war;
To-day, our veteran armies are abandoned,
Others reduced to paucity; severe
And sad our naval history; the states
Of all the South by Sherman's great Sea March
Are ravaged ; Richmond,—hope's proud citadel—
Must soon be prey to the relentless Grant—

 *Benj.*  All, all for self-agrandizement, for fame,
    *Re-enter* DAVIS.
To sate the morbid appetite of Lincoln,
That demon, despot Lincoln.  But yesterday
His second presidential term began

By which the Abolition Party takes
Another four years' lease of life   As king,
There is none greater.   On throne imperial
He sits, and servants come and go in costume ;
Ten thousand officers knee-tribute bring ;
And money ? money ? he buys well-bred saints
With money.

    *Davis.*        Benjamin, hast thou ne'er read
In sacred writ of King Belshazzar, lord
Of Golden Babylon ?   Read it again—
His glory, power, and *death*—and think of Lincoln.
             [*Stepping to* LEE *who proceeds to leave.*]
And thou, O noble son of Light-Horse Harry,
Do honor to thy father's dust !   This State
Which he did rule, which gave thee birth, oh serve
It well —Good-bye, good-bye.        [*Exit* LEE.
    The bull-dog grit of Grant will not surpass
The cunning of Lee's generalship.   Drawn on
By wiles, let Grant beguile himself till we
Complete our blessed cold-blood theme—our plot.
                [*Looks at his watch.*]
Within the leaguing den of death, this hour
Conspirators repair to whet their scythes
For mowing abolition's meadow.—Come,
We will be with them, come.      [*Exeunt.*

----

ACT IV.   SCENE II.   CONSPIRATORS' ROOM.

*Enter* BOOTH, HAROLD, ATZEROTH, PAYNE, THOMPSON *and* CLAY.

    *Thomp.*   Trained men I see you are, not late, nor yet
Ahead of time ; precision is the law
Of military schools, twice needful too
It is to those who mean to fight the kings.
Booth, Harold, Atzeroth, Payne, draw well the reins
Which guide your wills, that when the God of Time
From Heaven's belfry-clock shall give alarm
No thought can intervene between its sound
And *Liberty.*

    *Booth.*  They're skilled in use of knife,
And true to me, true as my name is Booth

The son of Brutus—Junius Brutus Booth—
Whose playing English actors envied ; who bred
In me a love for tragedy, and taught
Me when a boy to hold the dagger thus.          [*Draws dagger.*

   *Clay.*   The name ?   Thy father's name ?

   *Booth.*                    The name ?   His name ?
Junius Brutus as I told you,—name ?
It matters not, there's nothing in a name.

   *Thomp.*   It matters much.   The history of him
Whom Brutus slew you know.

   *Booth.*                    Aye, well !
Imperator, prefect, consul and dictator ;
Held sacredly divine his body—body
Which was the ravisher of women's virtue ;
Tyrannic lord, whom senators did guard,
And when he said *aha* they knelt in dust
To kiss the coin which bore his portrait.
So much like him is Lincoln grown that, by
The Brutus sire of me, and the Brutus
Who last thrust glittering steel in Cæsar's side,
And by the God supreme, in modern style
By leaden ball I'll end this tyrant's days.

   *Clay.*   The days which should have ended when before
Thou mad'st the trial, four years ago.

   *Thomp.*   (To CLAY) In this you speak it right.   This purse you
         (*to Booth*) take
Again, and foreman be to bloody deeds.
To you, and you, and you, (*Payne, Atz. and Har.*) for minor work
One half the sum was bargained.          (*Gives them purses.*)
       (*All clasp hands in a ring.*)
          Now clasp hands
And swear when the long-roll by you is heard
Every one will quit himself a man.

   *All.*   We swear.

   *Thomp.*   My noble fellows, farewell !
              [*Exeunt* THOMP. *and* CLAY.
   *Booth.*   My men, at dame Surratt's in Washington
Where we so lately were, we'll find a home
Till we can execute our sweet designs.          [*Exeunt.*

ACT IV.  SCENE III.--Davis' Cabinet Room.

*Enter* Davis *and* Benjamin.

*Davis.*  To-morrow night the President's *levee'*
Will bring congratulations to us all,
So skillfully we've made Richmond's defense.

*Benjamin.*  Will Lee be present.

*Davis.*                        He will.

*Benjamin.*                        We'll tell him then,
You, he, and I support this government
As pillars to an edifice

*Davis.*                Indeed, the truth.
I give commands and you subscribe your name,
While he does execution.  (*Aside*) Puppets you see.--

*Benjamin.*  Meade he defeated yesterday.

*Davis.*                        And Grant
Will get the worst of it to-day.—Last night
I—I—I showed Lee where to make attack.
                (*In praying style.*)
Virginia, O Virginia, proud Virginia,
Mother of patriots and mother of statesmen,
Mother of warriors and mother of presidents,
Devoutly holy mother.—I—I've made
Thy capital the capital of states,
And thy pure holiness I've set my life
To guard lest it be plucked by violence
                (*Enter* Gregory.)
This hallowed Sabbath let thy people pray—

*Greg.*  Your honor!  (*Handing him a letter.*)

*Davis.*                Will you interrupt me?
        (Davis *snatches the letter, tears the wrapper and throws*
        *all upon the table.* Benj. *is astonished.  Exit* Greg.)
This hallowed Sabbath let the people pray
That God himself may bless conspirators
Who seek to rid us of that enemy,
That chief of enemies—Lincoln.
        (*Grasps the letter and instantly reading it, shouts--*)
                *Alarum!*
        (Greg. *and another servant enters.*)
Why stand you (*to* Benj.) here aghast?  Oh, would the world

Was ended! then hell would gorge itself with Lincolns,
Devils and imps would keep them company.—
My heart despairs. (BENJ. *approaches and reads message
        from* DAVIS' *hand.*)
                        From Lee, from Lee, from Lee.

   *Benj.* (*Reads*) "In several places my lines are broken,
Flee for your lives," signed "Robert Lee"--
It cannot be, and yet it is. Withal
'Tis best at such a time as this to move
Most quietly.

      *Davis.*        Secretly?

      *Benj.*                      No, quietly—
Without excitement.

      *Davis.* (*Excitedly*) Yes, to Danville then.—
Have we no time to spoil this room?—Gregory,
The contents of the vault make haste to put
Aboard the train. [*Exeunt servants*]—what valuables are here?
None? You take these (*Hands* BENJ. *a confused mass of papers*)
                        My books! This chair must go
In honor to him who used it.
        (*Throwing an armful of books, proceeds to drag it off.*)
                        This's enough. (*Takes a book or two.*)
Wait for that rubbish? No!—To our departure.        [*Exeunt.*

-----

ACT IV.  SCENE IV.--IN THE FIELD—SUBURBS OF RICHMOND.
                (*Played on the Wing of the Stage.*)
                *Enter* LEE, EWELL *and attendants.*

   *Lee.* Richmond shall not detain us.—Fire depots,
Flour-mills, and all warehouses of tobacco;
Blow up the river-rams and other shipping;
To Danville then command our retreat, and burn
The bridges after you.                        |*Exeunt.*
                *Enter* GRANT *and* OFFICERS.

   *Grant.* Richmond's ablaze, and where is Lee? We must
Be stepping 'gainst his heels. On with the chase!
A week at most and he is ours.                |*Exeunt.*

ACT IV. SCENE V. Davis's Cabinet Room—Deserted.

*Enter* WEITZEL, LINCOLN *and* ATTENDANTS.

(*After the evacuation* LINCOLN *enters* RICHMOND, *and* W., *who is in command, shows him around.*)

*Weitzel.* The room so lately occupied by Davis—
His cabinet room, deserted as he left it.

*Lincoln.* With its desertion, hearts beat happily
Throughout the Nation, North and South; for here
Since '61 has Treason made his home.
Now, through the clouds the sun of Peace is breaking:
When Lee surrenders—a day or two from this—,
And Johnson—who then can't long endure—
Lays down his arms, that sun, that peaceful sun,
Will shine again in beauty on the Union.
Upon the streets I next would go, and then
To Libby Prison; thence to the hospitals—
I wish to see the soldiers, those who fought
The battles of our country, especially those
Who've fought at Richmond.

*Weitzel.* Return in this direction.          [*Exeunt.*

---

ACT IV. SCENE VI. In the Field.

(*Played on the Wing of the Stage.*)

*Enter* LEE *and* STAFF OFFICERS.

*Lee.* My army's been victorious and proud,
But, with its leader, it is humbled now—
'Tis fled, I fear, into its last extremity;
Unclothed the men are cold, unfed they're sick,
Unarmed they're weak, unpaid they're down in heart—
              *Enter* MESSENGER.
You bring what word?

*Mess.*              Sir, Sheridan's surprised
The train that brought supplies, and captured it
This hour he forms his cavalry in line
Across our front while yet behind these horsemen
Are seen his hosts, great hosts of infantry.
              *Enter* SECOND MESSENGER.
*Lee.* And you, what word?

*2d Mess.*                 Sir, Grant stands in battle line
Across our rear, but with no sign of action ;
Our army's faced both east and west —the east
To Grant, the west to Sheridan—

*Lee.*                     'Tis right,
Though it is vain to draw the contest closer.
There's honor in capitulation to which
I'll lead my men,  Return each one of you
With this command :  The army shall remain
Faced as it is in both directions ;
Let other music cease, but drums shall beat
A slow and martial tread while he steps forth
On either side to plant the flag of white —
Run, run, my messengers.              [*Exeunt Messengers.*
     The terms of the surrender I'll accept,
And you shall be the men to make the roll
Of officers and private soldiers.
     (*Behind the scenes on each side of the stage, drums are heard.*)
Oh, I must give it up !  Lead me, lead me out,
Yes, lead me out before my veteran corps
That I may grasp again the hand of *Warriors*,
That I may see once more their honest faces
While there my tongue shall say *farewell.*
Oh, lead me out.                     [*Exeunt.*
     [ *Two officers are locked arms with him and all go out.*

---

ACT IV.   SCENE VII.   THE PROMENADE.

*Enter* MR. AND MRS. LINCOLN, *arm in arm.*

*Mrs. L.*  I am very glad if cares do not too much
Involve you.—What time before—so long
It seems—had we an hour alone, do you
Remember ?

*Lincoln.*  No, Mary.  But henceforth for us
There're brighter days.  A peaceful future dawns,
When fewer duties will be mine, and I
Will know again the pleasures of your company.
     April fourteenth by calendar :  Sumpter
Was fired, and war began four years ago ;
To-day Fort Sumpter's flag's replaced, and war

Is almost ended,—Johnson sues for terms,
Lee has surrendered, and Davis fled.
The Union asks these erring back as treats
A father with his wayward son returning ;
Then the labor of my office's done ;
E'en now, you've heard the chimes of joyful bells,
Music's sweet rhythm, and cannons heavy boom—
Proud heralds of that long expected morn ;
You've seen the festooned streets, the bonfire's glare,
And the triumphal march of armies,—all
Emblazoned ensigns of my honor—
And you, you are my wife.

   *Mrs. L.*                    And you, my husband,
May wear these honors which so well would grace
A king.  But let me check your joyousness
Lest it portend some ill.

   *Lincoln.*              What ? ill ? design?
That is an idle fear, permit it not.—
A merry heart ! the theatre goes to-night,
And we shall be its foremost guests ; of us
The theatre shall buy a leisure hour—              [*Exeunt.*
  (*Mr. and Mrs. Lincoln, Miss Harris and Maj. Rathbone now
occupy private box on the right wing of the stage, the cur-
taining being closed until the beginning of Scene IX.*)

---

### ACT IV.  SCENE VIII.—A Dark Woods.

*Enter* BOOTH *and* HAROLD.

*Harold.*  (*Rubbing his face*) `
My countenance I'll mask with midnight black
Till it can tell no tale on Harold

  *Booth.*  Oh, fy ! that fighting-cocks must gablocks wear !
To ease the gout put medicine in the mouth ;
To cool a fever, do the same ; and if
The brain lack courage, here, here is the stuff
    (*Hands him bottle of whisky.*)
That'll give a motor-power to murd'rous hands
And change a civil face into a savage,—
   (BOOTH *produces another bottle and both drink.*  BOOTH
*gurgles the whisky in his throat.*)

Oh let it gurgle there till night is past
And worlds have seen an honest tragedy.—
　Harold, when *ten-ten* the theatre shall resound
Then, by the gods, be ready!　　　　　　　　　　　[*Exeunt.*

---

### ACT IV.　SCENE IX.—THE STAGE.

(*The curtains to Lincoln's private box are now drawn aside.*)

　　*Enter* OLD LADY *followed by* LORD SQUILLS.

　　*Old L.*　(*Askance*) You are the lord you say, then who am I?

　　*Lord S.*　His lady.

　　*Old L.*　　　　　　　Yes, yes! *old lady*—woman!
Ten years your senior makes me old--too old
I grant, to be your servant.　Not *again*
Will I be yoked to one so much my junior.　　　　[*Exit.*

　　*Lord S.*　Ha, Ha! she's counting on *another*, see?--
*I* am her fourth.—I called her *angel* once;
She said that I was *Squills*--since then, *pet* names
I much dislike.—Sweet babe, Roxana Stark,
Roxana Stark--Electric spark, rechristened—

　　(*A voice behind the scenes sounds "Ten-ten." At the same in-
　　stant* BOOTH *shoots* LINCOLN, *and jumping over the rail-
　　ing upon the stage, falls; but regains himself, and
　　making toward* LORD SQUILLS *who is scared from the
　　stage, secures his escape by a rear passage-way. A man
　　rushes up from in front. "Hang him!" and other cries
　　are heard.*)

　　*Booth*　(*Still in the box.*)　*Sic semper tyrannis!*
　　　　(*He jumps upon the stage and falls.*)

　　*Mrs. Lincoln.*　O! O God! My husband!

　　*Miss H.*　O, O, O!

　　*Rathbone.*　(*Grasping at Booth*) Hold! Help!

　　*Booth.*　(*On the stage and brandishing a large knife, while
　　　　making toward Lord S., who runs.*)
The South shall be free!　　　　　　　　　　[*Curtain drops.*

# ACT V.

## SCENE I--POLICE STATION.

*Enter* CHIEF OF POLICE *and* ASSISTANTS.]

*Chief.* (*Lieut. Baker.*) Thank God my men that Lincoln is
not dead.
The wretch that shot him, who may he be?
To find him out's my business.—Stand outside
You two and answer all who throng the door.—[*Exit Nos. 1 and 2.*
Ten minutes since the deed, and I must hear—
Bring thou the news.                              [*Exit No. 3.*
       (*To No. 4*) Go let the wires talk fast
And send the news to every point. [*Exit No. 4.*] He caught,
Must be in charge before the morning breaks.- -
(*To No. 5, a sec'y*) Write thou a Proclamation to Police :—
Call out the specials, mount one half of them,
And leave no place unsought.

### *Enter* No. 1.

*No. 1.* More help! the people of the streets are wild ;
Too like unbridled steeds they snuff the air,
And in excitement prick their ears to catch
The jargon of confusion.                          [*Exit.*

### *Enter* No. 4.

*No. 4.*                    Without is he
Who says the telegraph is cut in many places.--
No one answers to his call

### *Enter* No. 3.

*Chief.* (*To No. 3.*)  Returned? what word?

*No. 3.* Lincoln survives, but is unconcious ;
The ball has pierced his brain, a fatal shot.

       (CITIZEN *rushes in pursued by* No. 2.)

*No. 2.* Hold, man, hold!

*Citizen.*                    Hold, I cannot hold.

*Chief.*                                    Let'm speak—
No man runs thus to find a penny- -speak.

*Citizen.* Seward is stabbed, and Frederick his son.

*Chief.* Good God, what great conspiracy is this ?

*Citizen.* Seward lay sick with fever. Thrice his neck
Was thrust. The ruffian fled, and at the door
Was met by Frederick whom he felled,
Then made escape.

*Chief.* He shall repent the deed
Stern justice cannot poise her scales at this.

[*Exit No. 2 with Citizen.*

*No. 3.* My chief, 'tis thought their rendezvous is known,
And thither are dispatched our officers.

*Chief.* (*To No. 4.*) Admit of no delay Bring Rathbone here,
And Hawk the actor.

*No. 3.* Hawk came with me and waits. He recognized
The man, calls him the Bengal tiger Booth
Whose lair is at the house of Dame Surratt—
A widow—where by day he rests secure,
And whence by night he prowls for human gore.
But this is he now coming.

*Enter* HAWK *and* No. 4.

*No. 4.* Hawk, the Chief.

*Chief.* The actor!

*Hawk.* Yes.

*Chief.* The coward!

*Hawk.* Braggart, stop!
If cowards actors are, and actors cowards,
Yourself be at your trade and catch that actor,
That coward, and that assassin Booth. One needs
But *run* to catch a coward —art good to run?

*Chief* Tut! trifle not the hour.—Describe this Booth.

*Hawk.* Yourself must know him—Booth, John Wilkes the actor.

*Chief.* John Wilkes! the son of Junius Brutus Booth?
It seems but yesterday since he a lad
The mother's fond caress received, when played
Upon his cheek the gentle flush which youth
And kisses make. Then she arranged the curls
Of jet which graced his alabaster brow
And, smiling with a mother's love, was proud
That from her life had sprung this form, this face

Of innocence and beauty. Again she smiled
To see him step upon the stage to play
The tragedies his father'd taught him :
And for this latest living tragedy
The stage must take the blame— it plucked his heart
And put a viper there.—
　　(*To No. 4.*)　　This man attend
And at the court make bonds for reappearance.
　　　　　　　　　　[*Exeunt No. 4. and Hawk*
　　*Enter* Officers *with* Payne *and* Mrs Surratt.
(*Payne is without coat, clothes torn, and bespattered with mud ; wears a
cap made of a cross-section of his undershirt. Mrs S. is well but com-
monly dressed.*)
　　*Officer.*　Sir, this Surratt is mistress of a house
Where we inquiring were when came this man
At dead of night to dig some ditch he said
She'd promised him. 'Tis plain he is a knave,
And counterfeits the trade ; for see, his hands
Are white and soft as any girl's, and here're
The trinkets of his pockets—tooth and nail brushes.
His name is Payne,—
　　*Mrs. S. (pleadingly)*　O, man, I know you, man ;
I know your office ; I know your laws ; and as
A woman free of guilt I ask relief
And then protection.
　　*Chief.*　I grant protection now ;
Thy hearing, lady, must prove thy innocence.
(*To No. 3.*)　To penitentiary cells conduct them.
　　　　　　　　　　[*No. 3 and Sec's leads them out.*
　　*Mrs. S.* (*To Chief—savagely*) And now I know your heart.
　　　Abolition's black
Couldn't blacken it a whit !

　　*Payne.*　　　　　Curse ! curses, curse !

　　*No. 3.*　Come, come !　　[*Exeunt officers and prisoners.*

　　*Chief*　Murders and mysteries unlock themselves
With their own keys.—

　　*Officer.*　　　　　This evidence convicts them

　　*Chief.*　Accomplices, no doubt. But the assassin's name
Is Booth—was recognized by Hawk the actor—
We'll talk with him to put us on the track.　　[*Exeunt.*

## ACT V. SCENE II. POTOMAC RIVER.

*Enter* HAROLD *and* BOOTH.

(*Around the wing of the stage,* HAROLD *passes, soon followed by* BOOTH *hobbling on his crutches. They pass to the rear where they take the boat. By an opening of the scenes the river is made to appear*)

*Booth.* O Harold, I must stop again to rest.
Come back, and wait a bit!
    (*Booth sits and holds his ankle. Harold, running, returns.*)
                    I say, Harold,
It hurts me mightily.

*Harold.*            But stop not here,
Let's make the boat—'tis just around this bend;
Put on your coat and we ll be off.
    (HAROLD *has been carrying* BOOTH'S *coat and now assists him to put it on.*)
                  There now,
Where's your cane?—I'll help you on.
      [*They proceed to the boat.* HAROLD *takes the oar.*]

*Booth.* (*Crossing*) Truly, the Gods do favor us.—but hark!
                         [*Exeunt.*

---

## ACT V. SCENE III. PETERSON'S PARLOR WHERE LINCOLN DIED.

*Enter* STANTON, MADAM PETERSON *and* SERVANT.

*Stanton.* Madam, the room is well my choice. The couch
Place here in front of this uncurtained window,
That entering through its panes the morning sun
May kiss our dying father's lips, and leave
An answering farewell smile upon his cheek.

*Madam P.* As you ask, it shall be done.—Be done.(*to serv.*)
                        [*Exit servant.*

*Stanton.* Hither, by us whose hearts are warm in love
For him, will he be borne that sympathy
From our stout health, the virtue of a Christ
May be to make him whole.       [*Exit Stanton.*
    (*Enter* SERVANTS *with the couch.*)

*M'd Peterson.* Turn it more slightly toward the sun.—'Twill do.

'Tis all we can—they come.                    [*Exeunt.*

(*Enters* MEMBERS OF CABINET *bearing* LINCOLN *on a mat-
tress.* DR. ABBOTT *and* REV. DR. GURLEY *accompany them.*)

*Dr. Abbott.*  (*Marking pulse.*) His head raise gently.—The
pulse is very faint.

(STANTON *at the head, raises it.*)

*Stanton.*  Will not our fervent prayers avail ?

*Dr. A*                                    Too late.

*Stanton.*  Ah, no! not possible that hope is fled.

*Dr. A.*  His pulses cease.--Our father yields his spirit,
And life's extinct.

*All.*  (*Groans*) Oh, Oh!

*Stanton,*  We with our our priest will join in supplication.

(REV. DR. GURLEY *prays and all respond.*)

*Dr. G.*  Almighty God, with whom do live the lives
Of Thy departed faithful world; by whom
Their souls are crowned with honor at Thy throne
Where glory lights the brow, and happiness
The heart,—to Thee, O Thou the God of man,
Imperial Father, Sovereign Supreme,
We give Thee thanks that--though in grief we're bowed
To see our bless'ed Lincoln die a martyr—
He lived to know himself the Union's Savior,
And that, like Chist upon the cross, he closed
His eyes on *victory*.  His spirit's now
With Thee, where at Thy will celestial choirs
Shall sing his triumph.
                    Oh Thou Eternal One,
The great affliction of this hour grant us
The fortitude to bear    Let friends condole
With friends, and heaven no sympathy restrain ;
To us, as to this righteous-ruling king
May death consummate all our hopes in bliss
And everlasting joy.—Amen.

*Stanton.*  (*Bending over the body of* LINCOLN.)
My life, O Lincoln in exchange for thine—
                    (*All aside but Stanton.*)
We can no longer comfort life, we'll do

The honors to the dead. This sacred form
And couch, oh let me veil.

   (*The servants screen it from the audience by an upright black
curtain, behind which Dr. A. and Rev. G. disappear.*)

   *1st Cab. Mem.*   He is the strongest of us all —I'd have
Him speak to us. Speak to us, O Stanton!

   *Stanton.*   My colleagues, silence better suits the hour;
And yet, ye men, it is no time for silence,
Last week, the bells rang merrily, and joy
Fashioned the earth a newly-molten globe
Itself resplendent,—the end of war was come.
Last night, the bells tolled mournfully, for sorrow
Had bathed the earth with tears from every heart
That loved the Union,—this screen will tell the tale.
The Nation reels, so bloody is the crime.
Stand ye here like stocks, and seek no vengeance?

   *1st Cab. Mem.*   O South! the wicked South!

   *All.*                            We'll be avenged.

              (*They start to leave.*)

   *Stanton.*   No, No! enkindle not a flame of wrath
'Gainst all the South. Conspiracies are known
To only few.—These few will find them out
And then—

   *All*     We'll be avenged.   (*Start to go again.*)

   *Stanton.*                No, stay! No need—
Booth, the arch assasin, has conspired
With rebel leaders—'tis known, and well;
Both he and all his fiendish crew are chased
And hotly pressed,—No need that you should run
Indeed, you do not understand the times; –
Our Nation is without a government;
By right of office Johnson takes takes the chair
Of President, and we must see 'tis done—
Now come with me. We'll bear away the body.

   (*They pass behind the screen, et exeunt. A servant follows and
carries the screen.*)

ACT V.  SCENE IV.  GARRETT'S BARN.

BOOTH *and* HAROLD *asleep.*

*Each has two revolvers, and Booth a carbine.   Noise behind the scenes.
They talk in under-tone.*

*Harold.* (*rising*)  Booth !

*Booth.* (*suddenly waked*)  What ?

*Harold.*  Hear all that noise?—we're caught.      [*They rise.*

*Booth.*  Prepare yourself.  Stand still and hold your tongue.
Take your revolvers—there, that's the way.
[*Harold takes a revolver in each hand.  Booth leans on his crutch-
es and holds carbine.*]
Mark you, we'll stand them off.  We will—

*Chief.*  (*Outside*)  Ho, ho ! ye men within this barn, ho, ho !

*Booth.*  Be quiet ; hold your peace.  But guard the door,
And shoot the man that enters.

*Chief.*  Ye men, we send to you your landlord's son.
Give him your arms, and you yourselves come out,
Or we will burn the barn.       [*H. prepares to guard the door.*

*Booth.*  Withhold.  Don't shoot.
                    [*Young Garrett is pushed within.*

*Garrett.*  The soldiers, Booth, are here—they want you both—

*Booth.*  Young man, get out of here !

*Garrett.* (*backing toward the door*)  They'll burn the barn—

*Booth.*  You have betrayed us.  Damn you, out of here !
                    [*Garrett rushes through the door.*
Now Harold, now be brave.       [*H. stands guard again.*
                    I'll peer into
The darkness of the night and see who's come.
        [*Booth hobbles to the side of the barn to look.*

*Chief.*  Ho, ye ! you must surrender.

*Booth.* (*loudly*)  Who are you ?  What d'you want ?

*Chief.*  No difference who.  We know you.  Come out.
(*Harold trembles with fear.  He has sheathed his revolvers
and is unbuckling them when Booth turns.*)

*Booth.*  And you've laid down your arms ! d'you mean to flunk?
Have you a baby's heart, and pigeon's liver ?
Leave me, you arrant coward ; leave me, fool,

Else I will shoot you like a dog.  Leave me !

> [HAROLD *backs to the door, which is locked.*

*Harold.*  Oh, let me out—

*Chief.*                Give up your arms.

*Harold.*  I have no arms—Let me out—quick !

> [ *The door is opened and Harold jerked out.*

*Booth.*  (*Having examined Harold's revolvers puts them down.*)

I know my time is short, but do not fear—
I welcome death
          I've served  my country well ;—
The South was humbled by the war ; in it
The North exulted.—Sorrow brings sympathy
Which puts the arm of love around an enemy.    [*He prays.*
Father, grant me escape, or speedy death.

*Chief.*  Last warning ! without parley surrender !

> [ *The barn is fired—tableau.*

*Booth.* (*defiantly*)  You've caught me, Captain, but alive

You'll never take me.

(*Report of pistol.*  BOOTH *straightens to fullest height and falls.*
CHIEF BAKER *and* GARRETT *rush in to his assistance* )

> [*Curtain drops.*

---

NOTE.—The drama is so arranged that several characters may be represented
by the individual actors, as follows :
  Seward, Abbott.
Thompson, Chief of Police, Lee, Ghost of Henry.
Davis, Ghost of Washington, Rathbone.
Sanders, Donald, McPherson.
Stanton Grant, Clay, Taney.
Cameron, Bowen, Ewell, Cleary.
Stephens, Beauregard, Weitzel, Burnbridge, Squills.
Benjamin, Gurley, Tucker.
Lady Lincoln, Madam Peterson.
Lady Davis, Miss Harris,
Mrs. Surratt, Mrs. Squills.

www.ingramcontent.com/pod-product-compliance
Lightning Source LLC
Chambersburg PA
CBHW031322280626
47169CB00019B/2640